**The Hombeez are proud to be members of
The Partnership for a Drug Free America.**

BOOKS

Hangin' with the Hombeez...The Spelling Bee
© 1997 Noware Productions/ Dann Gershon and David Robinson

For information regarding permission, please write to:
Noware Productions, email: NOWARE @ aol.com

Library of Congress Catalog Card Number
97-092875
ISBN 0-9656985-3-X
Printed in Singapore

Hangin' With The Hombeez

The Spelling Bee

Story by Dann Gershon

Drawings by David Robinson

As his hombeez flew to school
B Cool stayed home...being cool.
He played hookey and that's a fact.
The whole hive thought B Cool had cracked.

B Cool's hombeez came to study
With their nutty, little buddy.
But, he just watched as the three
Studied for the spelling bee.
"Wanna know what makes me sick?
Spelling and arithmetic.
But, if I'm up against a wall
I like spelling least of all!"
"Wake up!" they said to his face.
"Where's your head? In outer space?"

B Cool laughed and ignored their pleas,
"Spelling is useless you dumb bumble beez.
School is for fools.
I have nothing to learn.
I'll break all the rules
And burn them in turn.
Listen y'all,
Let's do something groovy
Let's fly to the mall
And see a B movie."

B Cool waited in the line
But failed to see a brand new sign.
"NO FREEBEEZ" it quite clearly stated.
The sign was even signed and dated.
The ticket taker pointed down
And calmly said, "Move it, clown.
I suggest you come back, Sonny
When you have a little honey."
B Cool shouted, " I'm no slob.
I'll go out and get a job!

The King said, "Cool, make no mistake.
I sell the sizzle. Not the steak.
"Wanna be rich like me?
Start off as an errand bee."

There's a box in the rear
By the two cuckoo clocks.
You can smell it from here.
It's chock full of lox.
So deliver the box.
After all, it's your duty."
"Head for the docks.
Go on...Shake your booty!"

B Cool tried to deliver
The box of lox
And ended up lost
In the Beeford boondocks.
Suddenly, a voice
Came from out of thin air
And offered Cool no choice
But to drop the lox there.
"You heard me," said the voice,
"I said drop that box, Buster"
And out walked a wasp in a long, yellow duster.

The argument grew
As arguments do.
Until B Large bellowed,
"Are you two quite through?
Stop it! Stop it! Stop it! Stop it!
This is dumb. Why don't you drop it?
How would you boys like to have a hoot
And get to test your wits to boot?
That's the answer. Don't you see?
A good old fashioned spelling bee."

The wasp agreed that it was best
To settle it with a spelling test.
As they watched him fly away,
B Cool had a few things to say.

"B Large," he whispered. "I must confess
This truly is a great big mess
The time has come for me to tell
I really need to learn to spell."
B Cool got down on his knees
And pleaded, "Help me! Help Me!"

"Help Me, Please!"

"There's a machine called a Gizmo
Invented by a bee in Pismo.
I hook it up to your head,
Then I send you off to bed
And as you sleep, you learn to spell
That's the Gizmo! Ain't it swell?"

But, the Gizmo was a little tight
And B Cool didn't sleep all night.
He didn't sleep, he didn't learn.
All he got was a little burn.

B Large said, "Rap is a snap."
As his toes began to tap.
"Learn to rap and you can spell.
That's why rap is so XL!
Let's play the song, loud and strong,
And we can both sing along."

They soon were jamming
In an off beat key.
And forgot about cramming
For the spelling bee.

"The answer," hummed Hunnie
Is perfectly clear.
It's really not funny,
I'm being sincere.
Start by learning your ABC's
And spelling will be such a breeze.
Isn't that simple? So plain too see?

Excuse me, fool. Are you listening to me?"

B Cool said nothing. Not even a peep.
It seems he was snoring,
Deep asleep in a heap.

Queen La Tee B was known
For her secret lotions,
Brews made from bones
And magical potions.
She sang as she stirred
A pitted old pot.
Then the old bird asked,
"Are you ready? Or not?"

"Alphabet soup?" sighed B Cool
As he stared at the brew.
"There must be more that you can do!"

He stopped and he stood
On a step on the stoop
And looked at the letters
In his alphabet soup.
"Look at the letters!"
B Cool shouted with glee
"There's an A and a B
And a C and a D.
Every little letter from A to Z.
Look at the letters!
Letters spell words!
Spelling is great!
It's not just for nerds."

Mrs. Beebody explained
The rules to the group.
As B Cool drained
His alphabet soup
"I'll have no belching or biting
During my spelling bee.
There's no farting or fighting."
Or you'll answer to me."

Then she added in a mumble,
"It's showtime y'all,
Let's get ready to bumble!"

But where was the wasp?
Was he going to show?
Could the wasp be lost
Or caught in the snow?

As B Cool refilled his bowl to the brim.
He saw the wasp and the wasp saw him.
In the back of the room,
Near to the rear
His face filled with gloom,
Eyes beginning to tear.
B Cool could tell
That all was not well.
Then he knew...the wasp couldn't spell.

"I know I have lost.
I just can't hack it.
By the way," said the wasp
I'm a yellow jacket."

Cool gave the yellow jacket a hug
And said, "Between you and me, just bug to bug.
We did not lose in the end
Because we both made a friend.
I think we should go back to school.
I think that school is really cool.

Stop by sometime and we can study.
I'll make some soup. How 'bout it, buddy?

It'll be great. Just wait and see.
Next year we'll win that spelling bee."

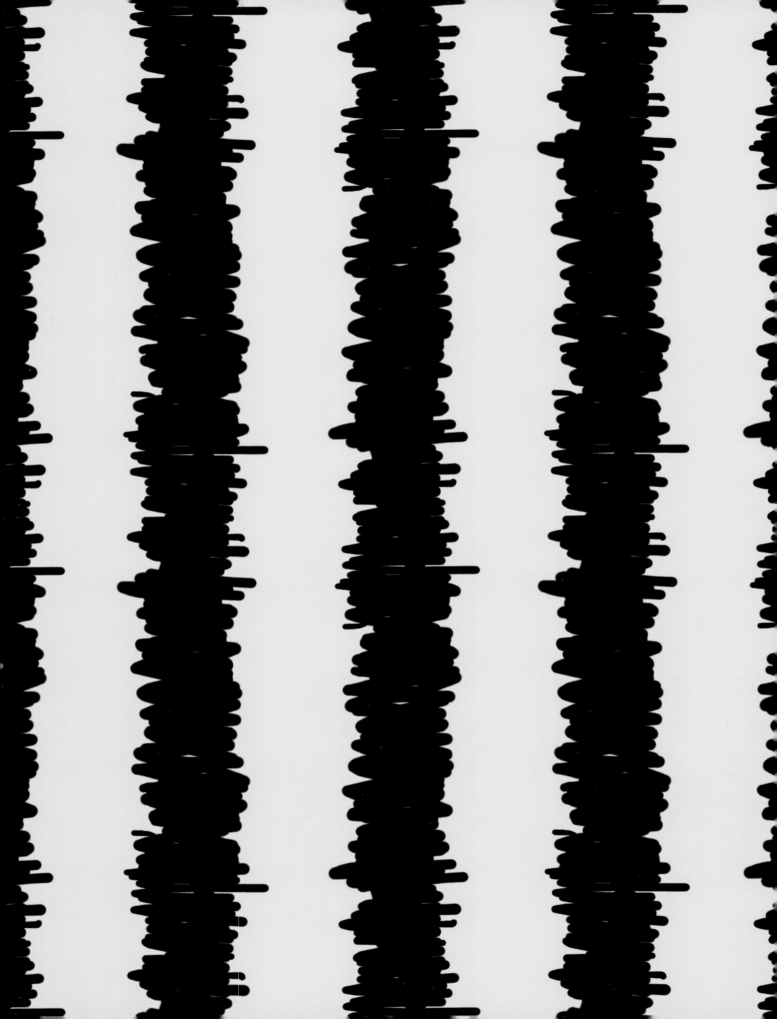